SMALL WALT

Story by **Elizabeth Verdick**

Pictures by **Marc Rosenthal**

SCHOLASTIC INC.

ISBN 978-1-338-36027-1

Text copyright © 2017 by Elizabeth Verdick. Illustrations copyright © 2017 by Marc Rosenthal. All rights reserved. Published by Scholastic Inc., 557 Broadway, New York, NY 10012, by arrangement with Simon & Schuster Books for Young Readers, an imprint of Simon & Schuster Children's Publishing Division. SCHOLASTIC and associated logos are trademarks and/or registered trademarks of Scholastic Inc.

12 11 10 9 8 7 6 5 4 3 2 1   18 19 20 21 22 23

Printed in the U.S.A.   40

First Scholastic printing, December 2018

Book design by Lizzy Bromley
The text for this book was set in Archetype.
The illustrations for this book were rendered in Prismacolor pencil and digital color.

BRRRR, the night air is cold and wet.
The city plows stand in a row, ready to fight the snow.

There's Walt, the smallest snowplow in the fleet.
Maybe this time he won't get picked last.

"I'm not taking the little guy!" says Big Buck.
"Neither am I," says Hank. "He's too small for a big snow like this."

Walt waits and waits . . .

and waits.

"*I'll* drive him," says Gus.

Gus starts Walt up.

He checks Walt's load
of ice-melting salt.

He inspects the salt spreader—
switch, twist.

He tests the plow—
up, down—

and the lights—
off, on.

"Good to go," says Gus.

The other drivers head out first,
plow after plow after plow.
Fat snowflakes hit the windshield—
splat-splat—while Walt waits his turn.
Big Buck *HONK HONK*s.
"Try to keep up, Small Stuff!" he shouts.
Grrrr, Walt's engine growls.

Each plow has a route to follow.
Walt knows where to go.

First the bridges—icy!

Then the ramps—dicey!

Walt's tires grip the road—*rumble-grumble*.
His lights flash—*wink, blink*.
His plow pushes the snow—*scraaaatch, scraaaape*—
and his spreader scatters salt—*swoosh-whoosh*.

His engine hums:
My name is Walt.
I plow and I salt.
I clear the snow
so the cars can go!

The radio squawks: "Citywide blizzard!
Head home, folks. Head home!"
But snow-fighters work all-nighters. . . .

Sleet pelts Walt's windows.
The wind whips his sides.
Long lanes loom ahead.

Walt plows on, mile after mile after mile.
So much slush and muck!
Don't get stuck. . . . Don't get stuck.

His engine thrums:
My name is Walt.
I plow and I salt.
They say I'm small,
but I'll show them all.

Whoa! There's a hill ahead—a high, high hill.
"I've never seen such big drifts.
I don't think we're up to this," says Gus.
Walt slows.

Behind Walt, two bright headlights blaze.
It's Big Buck.

"We could let Buck plow the hill," says Gus.
Walt's engine revs. *Errr Vroom-vaRoom!*
"Okay," says Gus. "I hear you."

So up they go . . . up . . .
uuuup . . . uh-oh!

Walt's back end skids,
slips down,
down . . .

He shudders, sputters. But . . .
*A plow and salter
can never falter.
Plow and salter,
never falter.*

"Want to try again, Walt?"
VROOM-VROOM—VROOOOOM!
Gus hits the gas.

Walt climbs up, *up*, UP to the very tip, *tip* TOP where . . .

he stops.

Oh, that's a *looooooong* way down.

"You can do it, Walt!"
Not too small, not too small.
His engine drums:
We're Gus and Walt.
We plow and we salt.
We'll fight the snow.
Get ready—now GO!

Together they forge a path
down that steep, steep hill,
leaving a trail of salt—
and Big Buck—behind them.

"We did it, Walt!" says Gus.
Errrrnnnntttt! Hissss Yessssss.
Beep-beep!

At dawn—*YAWN*—Gus and Walt
head back to the lot.
Gus hollers hello.
Hank salutes.
And Big Buck says, "The little guy
did a better job than I thought."
ChuggaMmmm-hmmm!

Gus chuckles. Then he takes off his winter scarf
and ties it in a bow on Walt's rearview mirror.
"A blue ribbon for my buddy."
Walt's engine purrs.
Never faltered. . . . Never faltered.
Gus pats the dashboard and says good night.

The plows stand in a row, ready to fight the snow.
Small Walt is still the littlest in line,
but he's got a big blue ribbon . . .
and good old Gus.
"See you tonight, Snow-fighter!"